This book belongs to:

....

For Karim, who brought into my life many magical tales,
to live and to write about.
Nadine

American edition published in 2018 by Lantana Publishing Ltd., London, UK.
www.lantanapublishing.com

First published in the United Kingdom in 2016 by Lantana Publishing Ltd.
info@lantanapublishing.com

Text & Illustration © Nadine Kaadan 2018

Distributed in the United States and Canada by Lerner Publishing Group, Inc.
241 First Avenue North, Minneapolis, MN 55401 U.S.A.

For reading levels and more information, look for this title at
www.lernerbooks.com.

Printed and bound in Hong Kong.
Cataloging-in-Publication Data Available.

ISBN: 978-1-911373-27-8
eBook ISBN: 978-1-911373-31-5

The Jasmine Sneeze

NADINE KAADAN

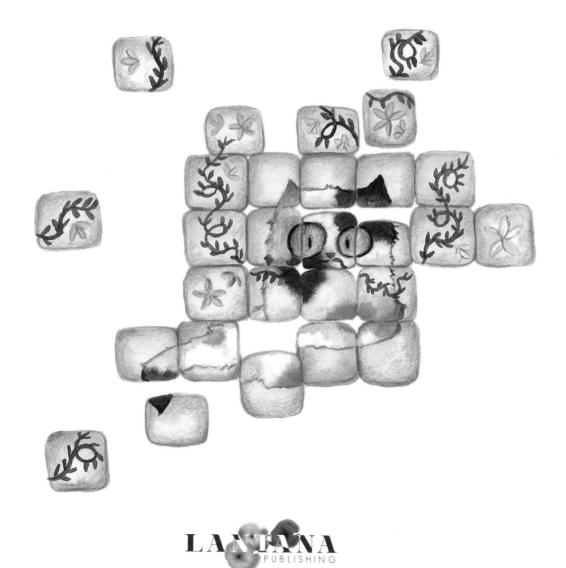

LANTANA
PUBLISHING

Haroun is the happiest cat in the world.
He lives in Damascus, the city of a million
and one cats. He spends most of his time
sleeping on the marble floor next to the
fountain in his favorite courtyard.

Sometimes he stays up late for a karaoke
party with the other cats in the moonlight.

Everyone loves cats in this city and people often stop to stroke Haroun. With every dinner party in the neighborhood, he is always the first to get a treat.

But life isn't easy. Oh no,
there is one thing that ruins
everything: jasmine!

Haroun can't stand the
sweet-scented flowers. Their
pollen makes him sneeze so
much that he can't sleep.

Haroun doesn't understand why people in Damascus love jasmine so much. They treat it as a member of their own family!

"Do you smell how lovely the jasmine is this evening?" Haroun hears his neighbor say to his daughter. "It must be celebrating your little sister's birth!"

"But this sneezy scent is spoiling my lovely summer nights as it drifts all around," Haroun thinks.

Not for long! He comes up with a crafty plan to fix it.

أبواب دمشق السبعة

Haroun finds the old fish skeleton from his dinner a few nights ago and puts it in the closest jasmine tree pot. "It smells so much better now!"

Then he goes to the next tree and carefully places chicken bones on its roots from his favorite butcher's bin. "Lovely!"

Soon enough, he has decorated every tree in his street with his beloved stinky smells. Happy with his night's work, Haroun settles down to sleep, certain that this time his nap will be free of the jasmine sneeze.

Little does he know that he has caught the attention of the Jasmine Spirit. No one has ever seen the Jasmine Spirit, but they say she has lived in the jasmine trees of Damascus for thousands of years.

And just when Haroun closes his eyes to take his precious nap beside the fountain, something very strange happens.

A stem of jasmine starts growing out of his nose!

What is this?! His very own jasmine tree? What a disaster!
Haroun starts sneezing and just can't stop!

The Jasmine Spirit has put a spell on
Haroun, so that every time he tries to sleep,
another jasmine stem grows out of his nose.

Sleep is impossible with all this jasmine
creeping from his nose, sending him into
fits of sneezes!

Haroun tries his hardest to pull the stems out, but that only makes his sneezes louder!

He thinks that the flowers might hate cold water as much as he does, so he jumps into the water fountain, only to find that jasmine loves water and grows even more!

Haroun hears giggling, and realizes that it is the Jasmine Spirit up to her tricks!

But what can he do?

Yowling miserably, he runs back to the first tree, hoping that for once the Jasmine Spirit will let herself be seen, but he can't find her.

He only finds the antique shop owner staring at the flowers by the front door.

"My jasmine smells terrible this morning!" Haroun hears her say. "It must know that my mother is unwell and is drooping in sympathy."

Haroun searches every tree for the Jasmine Spirit, but everywhere he looks, people seem worried about the jasmine's new smell. No one stops to stroke him, and even the butcher forgets to give him a treat.

"It wasn't like this when the jasmine smelled sweet and sneezy," Haroun thinks.

And in a flash, he knows what to do.

Hurrying back to every tree, Haroun removes the stinky snacks he has left there.

The work is hard under the hot Damascus sun. When he reaches the last tree, he is exhausted. He finds some shade under the jasmine branches and finally lays down his head to rest, too tired to care about the stems growing out of his nose.

Before long, he is fast asleep.

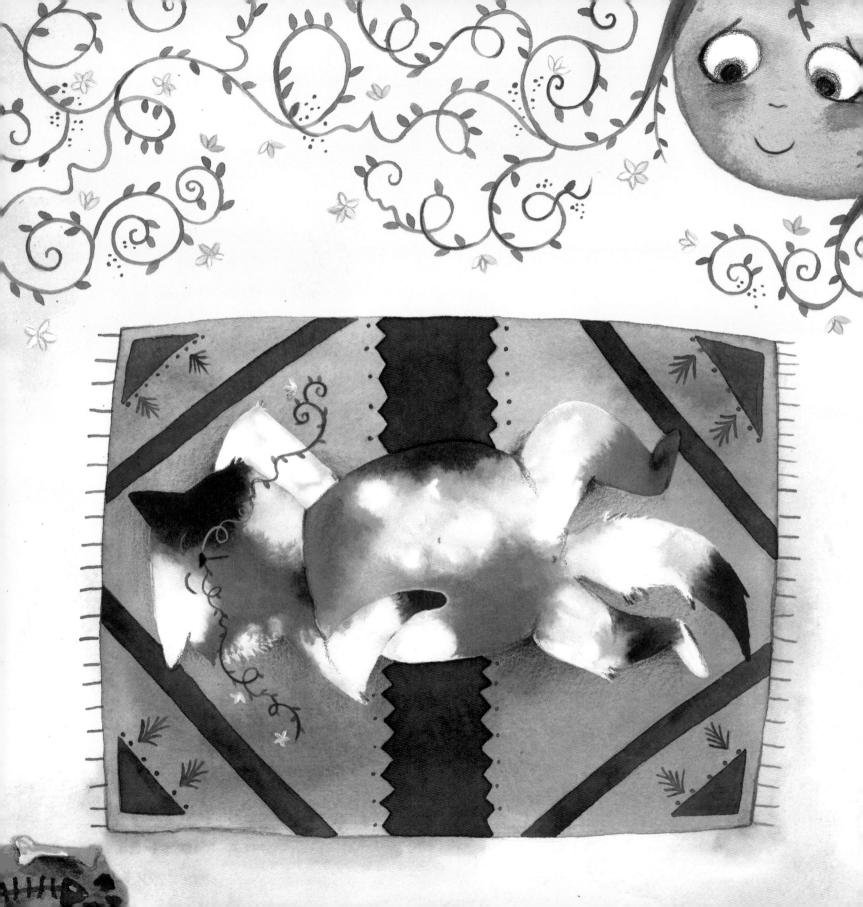

The Jasmine Spirit watches Haroun while he sleeps, and notices that many people smile when they see him. It seems that Haroun is much-loved, in spite of his untidy ways.

Since he has worked so hard to clean up his mess, she finally decides that he has learned his lesson and will never forget it.

When Haroun wakes up, he is surprised to see that the jasmine stems are gone and so are his sneezes. He has a good old stretch under the cool shade of the tree.

"It's not so bad sleeping beneath the jasmine," thinks Haroun.

Its leaves shade him from the sun, helping him to doze more deeply, and the smell isn't so irritating now that he's used to it.

Perhaps he just needed to give
it a chance.

The next day at nap time, Haroun curls up in the shade of the tree once more. He closes his eyes to sleep. The jasmine scent covers him like a blanket and makes him feel at peace.

For the first time, he realizes that he likes the jasmine smell.

"Maybe it means the Jasmine Spirit is watching over Damascus," he thinks sleepily. "Maybe..."

Damascus: the City of Jasmine

Locals know Damascus in Syria, the oldest capital city in the world, as the City of Jasmine. The sweet-scented jasmine flowers are a much-loved feature of the city's courtyards and ancient alleyways and give the city its distinct odor, especially on cool summer nights. As part of their morning ritual, Damascenes will wake and collect fallen jasmine flowers and place the petals on their water fountains so that the smell can be carried all over the house.

Many people in Damascus like to believe that the jasmine tree reflects what is happening in their homes and lives, in good times and in bad. They often associate blooming jasmine stems with joy and celebration and drooping jasmine stems with grief and loss. When a member of a family passes away, it is believed that the jasmine mourns the lost loved one.

My mother used to tell me about her grandmother's jasmine tree. She speaks of how, a day before her grandmother passed away, the jasmine in their courtyard suddenly became harsh and wild, as though in warning that something sad was about to happen. When my mother's grandmother passed away, the jasmine died the day after.

I always thought that this old jasmine tale could inspire a wonderful children's book, and here it is!

Nadine Kaadan